Mother, Sister, Daughter

THEOPLYIS DASHER

NEWMAN SPRINGS PUBLISHING
320 Broad Street
Red Bank, NJ 07701

First originally published by Newman Springs Publishing 2024

ISBN 979-8-89308-316-3 (Paperback)
ISBN 979-8-89061-139-0 (Digital)

Printed in the United States of America

This book, which is my first project, is dedicated to my son Ryan Rashad Dasher (RIP) and my beautiful daughter Choyce.

Acknowledgments

I would like to thank God first and foremost for my life and life experiences.

Thank you to my father, Don, who has supported and encouraged me throughout my life.

A very special thank-you to my beautiful mother, Elmira, who has always been there for me through the ups and downs. I know your prayers and love have sustained me over the years.

Thank you to my sisters Ena and Shandrinke. I love you both.

To all of my extended family, thank you for the love.

To my 1987 classmates at T. R. Miller High School, I love you guys.

To my 1991 classmates and friends at Troy University, thank you all.

Thank you, Pastor Lance Campbell, for your amazing artwork.

Mother, Sister, Daughter is a compelling murder mystery that puts an adopted twin in jail for homicide. Susanna Logan is fighting for her freedom in a case of mistaken identity by a sister she never knew she had.

Lonnie and Melissa Logan were resting in their North Carolina home. They had just arrived back from a five-day honeymoon in Costa Rica. The newlyweds had decided to finally get married after two years of dating.

SSG Lonnie Logan of the United States Army had orders to go to Afghanistan. The deployment was scheduled for three years, but there could be a second tour depending on the war.

The lovebirds tried so hard on their honeymoon to conceive. All the pregnancy tests had come back negative. Melissa was hoping to conceive before Lonnie left so she wouldn't be alone. They only had five days until he left. They were both nervous and afraid, but Lonnie was assuring his new bride that he would return. Melissa had decided to go back to school to become a nurse and work part-time to stay busy.

As they were driving to the base, Melissa was crying and squeezing her husband's hand. As they entered the gates, they saw the big C-130 waiting along with soldiers' loading equipment.

"I'm going to miss you so much," Melissa cried out as she wiped her tears.

"Sweetheart, I know, and I'm going to miss you more," said Sergeant Logan as he pulled her close and kissed her on the forehead.

The phone rang. It was Melissa's mother, Mrs. Becker.

"Hi, Mom. I'm saying goodbye to Lonnie. I'll call you back." She turned back to Lonnie. "Lonnie, it's not fair that you leave me after we just got married."

"I know, honey, but we both knew it was coming."

"What if I'm pregnant?" asked Melissa frantically.

"Sweetheart, you have your parents. You know they will look after you, and I will call every chance I get."

They kissed passionately as if it was their first kiss.

"I love you so, so much, and I'm proud to call you my husband."

"I love you too, Melissa Logan. You have no idea."

They hugged tightly as if they would never see each other again. *Pow, pow, crackle* came the sounds of thunder as the rain came down harder. After kissing her once more, he grabbed his bags, tightened his hat, and made his way to the big monster that would take him thousands of miles away.

"I love you, Sgt. Logan!" she screamed with the window halfway down and rain bouncing off her face. As she rolled up the window, she could hear the massive engine start to roar and see the propellers start to turn. She began to cry all over again as she watched him enter the back of the plane. Other families were waving and crying. "It's just not fair," she whispered, wiping away tears.

The engines roared louder, and lights blinked. The C-130 started to move. Melissa wanted to drive away, but she couldn't until the plane disappeared. The plane took off, and she whispered a prayer, ending it with "Amen." At about that time, she felt something in her stomach that she never felt before.

"OMG!" she shouted as she rubbed her stomach.

The metal monster was racing down the runway and gaining speed. Melissa started to cry out of control as she beat the steering wheel in anger. The man she just vowed her life to had taken off and was disappearing into the rain and clouds. All she could see was the blinking red light as it faded with every blink. The other loved ones were exiting the base. As she looked up with blurred vision because of the tears falling as fast as the rain, she decided to crank up her car and join the slow-moving line of cars.

The phone was ringing. It was Melissa's mom again.

"Hold on, Mom. Let me pull over. It's raining really bad."

Melissa pulled into a convenience store that was packed with other cars waiting out the storm.

"Melissa, are you okay?" asked her mom.

"Yes, Mother, I'm okay."

"Well, why didn't you call me back? I'm worried sick."

"I was saying my goodbyes, and now it's raining something awful," Melissa explained.

"I saw the forecast on the news, saying that there was going to be bad weather," stated Mrs. Becker as she tried to remain calm.

"It's bad but not bad enough to cancel the flight," stated Melissa in a whimpering voice.

"Aww, sweetie, I know how you feel. I dealt with the same thing with your father," stated Mrs. Becker, trying to offer some comfort.

"Okay, Mother. I'm pulled into a store. I'm going to get coffee," said Melissa.

"Please call me when you get home, Melissa. I'm worried about you," asked her mother.

"Sure, Mom. Don't worry. I'll be fine. I love you."

Melissa found herself shaking hysterically as she tried to sip the hot coffee. While watching the slow-moving traffic and listening to the rain on the roof of her car, she thought back to the feeling she felt in her stomach, wondering if it could be.

After sitting for a while, Melissa grew restless. Her thoughts were racing, and were all based on fear. The phone pinged with a weather alert warning of severe flooding because of torrential downpours. The rain was not letting up, so Melissa decided to make her way home.

A normal twenty-minute drive turned into a forty-five-minute drive because of the slow-moving traffic and blinding rain. She started her car, put on her seatbelt, and continued to hold her coffee. As she eased out into traffic, fear gripped her, and she thought.

"This is what it's going to be like, fighting storms all alone." She started to whimper all over again as she sped up. With only a few miles to go until home, she finally felt a little relief. After sitting her coffee in the cupholder, she picked up her pinging phone and saw it was a text message from her mom, and *boom*! The airbags popped out of the steering wheel. Her face was buried, and her neck was snapped back. Her senses went blank, and everything was black. She was sitting there, lifeless, with her face buried in the airbag.

The onstar voice was repeating, "Are you okay? Are you okay?"

No response.

After a few minutes, she could hear sirens wailing and getting closer. She started to cry, holding her stomach. As the ambulance was weaving in and out of traffic, she was complaining about her neck and a headache.

A paramedic was now asking various health questions including one about pregnancy.

Melissa paused and answered, "I don't know."

While being wheeled into the emergency room, she was asking about her phone.

A paramedic answered her, "Your purse and phone is with the officer investigating the accident. He will be here soon.

"I need my phone. I need my phone please," she begged profoundly. "Nurse, please, I need my phone," asked Melissa again.

"Okay, ma'am, your phone will be here shortly. Please try not to move," explained the nurse.

Melissa grabbed her neck as she was being transferred from the gurney to the hospital bed.

"Hi, I'm Dr. Riley. How are you?"

"My neck hurts, and I really need my phone," said Melissa.

"Okay, we're going to do a few X-rays, and you can make any calls you need to make," explained the doctor.

*****

Sgt. Logan and the rest of the soldiers were stopping in Germany to unload equipment and pick up more. There would be an overnight layover, so Lonnie would get a chance to call Melissa.

*****

Melissa's mom was calling back to back. Officer Anderson was on the way to the hospital and saw the calls coming, identified as Mother. He wanted to answer but didn't know the condition of Melissa.

*****

"Mrs. Logan, your X-rays are negative, but I'm concerned about the swelling in your neck," explained Dr. Riley.

"I'm feeling drowsy. I need my phone," whispered Melissa with closed eyes.

"The nurse gave you something for pain, and the officer should be back in the ER with your phone," explained the doctor.

"Room 205 is ready, Dr. Riley," said the nurse.

"Okay, monitor her closely. I don't want her moving too much," instructed the doctor. "She may get excited when she gets her phone," he added.

"Yes, sir, and by the way, she is pregnant," advised the nurse.

"Does she know?" asked the doctor.

"She hasn't mentioned it," answered the nurse.

"If she doesn't mention it, let's not tell her until she is a little more stable," said the doctor.

"Okay, no problem," answered the nurse.

*****

Officer Anderson was waiting for Melissa to get back from her X-ray. Melissa's phone was ringing off the hook with video calls from an international number. There were seven calls back to back from Lonnie and thirty-one missed calls from her mom.

*****

Lonnie was thinking she might have gone home and fallen asleep. *The bad weather and anxiety has worn her out,* he thought.

*****

"Hello, Officer. I'm Dr. Riley. Are you investigating the Logan accident?"

"Yes, I am, Doctor," answered Officer Anderson.

"We're getting her stabilized in room 205," explained Dr. Riley.

"How is she doing?" asked the officer.

"She is going to be okay. We're monitoring her neck area. We gave her pain medication, so she is a little groggy but coherent," explained the doctor.

"Her phone is going crazy," said the officer.

"And she has been crazy about her phone," said the doctor. "She should be ready in a few, but check with the nurse before you go in. And by the way, she is pregnant," stated Dr. Riley.

"Okay, will do, Doc. Thanks for the info," said the officer.

"Hi, Ms. Logan. I'm sorry, is it Mrs. or Ms.?" asked Officer Anderson.

Struggling to answer because of a heavy dose of pain medication, Melissa responded, "I need to call my mother."

"It doesn't seem you are coherent enough to talk," said the officer. "Would you mind if I called her and placed the phone on speaker to help you?" asked the officer.

"Who are you?" she asked, confused.

The nurse walked in. "Is everything okay?" asked the nurse.

"She is really out of it," stated Officer Anderson.

"If she is not used to taking pain medication, a dose of morphine could really take her for a loop," explains the nurse.

"Can I come back tomorrow?"

"Yes, that would probably be best. Around noon," suggested the nurse.

"Lonnie, is that you?" mumbled Melissa.

"I'll go now," whispered the officer. Officer Anderson left Melissa's purse and phone with the nurse. The phone started ringing again, and the nurse hurriedly left the room so Melissa wouldn't hear it even though she appeared to be sleeping. The nurse secured the purse in the locker and took the phone to Dr. Riley as he would be the person to call the emergency contact.

"How are her vitals?" asked the doctor.

"They are good," answered the nurse.

"Okay, good. The swelling on her neck should be down by morning, hopefully, and we will do an ultrasound to confirm the pregnancy," stated the doctor.

Melissa's phone was ringing, and the caller ID read Mother.

"Hello, Mrs. Logan?" asked Dr. Riley.

"No, this is Mrs. Becker, Melissa's mother," said her mom. "Where is my daughter?" asked Mrs. Becker, angry and confused.

"This is Dr. Riley at UNC Health Rex Hospital. Melissa was involved in an accident and is doing fine," explained Dr. Riley.

"OMG, where is she now?"

"She is resting in the ER. There is swelling around her neck area, but her X-rays were negative," explained the doctor.

"Oh gosh, I'm on my way from Georgia. It'll be a few hours," said Mrs. Becker.

"Why don't you wait till morning? Visitation starts at 8:00 a.m.," explained the doctor. "There is nothing you can do, Mrs. Becker. She is on a heavy dose of morphine, so she won't know that you're there."

"Okay, Doctor, I'll take your word, but I will be there at 8:00 a.m. sharp," said Mrs. Becker.

"Sounds good. I look forward to meeting you, and don't worry. She will be fine," said the doctor.

Melissa was finally resting normally, and everything seemed to be fine. It was 2:00 a.m., and the nurse was recording vital signs. She checked the swelling, and it had gone down considerably, which was a good sign. She survived a hard impact without any major injuries. The next concern was to confirm the pregnancy.

*****

"Good morning!" Mrs. Becker greeted the receptionist as she entered the ER.

Mrs. Becker nervously walked down a short hallway, looking side to side at the patients. Some were hooked up to machines with wires stuck to their bodies, and others appeared to be sleep. The number 205 was displayed on a room to the right. The door was closed, and she could hear Melissa's voice. She walked in, and there was Melissa, sitting up on the bed. She looked fine, her mother thought with relief. She sat the flowers down and smiled. Melissa stood up and squeezed her mom tightly.

"You had me worried, Melissa."

They both grabbed each other simultaneously and hugged again. With tears rolling down their faces, they embraced as if they hadn't seen each other in years.

"I'm glad you're okay. How do you feel?" asked her mom.

"I'm okay, except my neck is a little sore."

"It looks like the swelling has gone down," said her mom as she examined Melissa's neck.

In came the nurse. "Hi, how are you?" greeted the nurse.

"Hi, I'm Melissa's mom," responded Mrs. Becker.

"Nice to meet you. Your daughter is super sweet," said the nurse as she started to examine Melissa's neck. "The swelling has gone down, and I know you are ready to go," said the nurse.

"You have no idea. I hate hospitals," said Melissa.

"There is one more thing we have to do before you leave," explained the nurse.

"What is that?" asked Mrs. Becker.

"We have to confirm if you're going to be a grandmother!" excitedly explained the nurse.

"Oh, didn't know you were pregnant, Melissa," said her mom with excitement.

"We don't know for sure, Mom," said Melissa with apprehension.

As Melissa and the nurse were walking down the hall for the ultrasound, Melissa was nervous and afraid. She wanted a baby but did not want to do it alone. With Lonnie gone, she was afraid of being a single parent. She often thought of him not returning from the war. If she was not pregnant, it wouldn't bother her too much.

As the nurse was rubbing the greased instrument over her stomach, they could see not only one but two little tiny bodies. "There they are," said the nurse, smiling.

"OMG, two babies?" asked Melissa as she covered her mouth in disbelief but also happiness. After seeing the two babies, all the negative thoughts she had disappeared as if they were never there.

"Looks like about six weeks old," said the nurse.

"He is going to be so excited," said Melissa about her husband.

"Where is he, if you don't mind me asking?"

"He is in Afghanistan. He left yesterday morning," said Melissa.

"Aww, that's too bad," said the nurse.

"It's okay. I have my parents, and he will have occasional furloughs," explained Melissa.

The nurse and Melissa start to walk back to the room when Melissa stops and ask the nurse not to tell her mom she is pregnant with twins. The nurse asked, "Why?"

Because it's a blessing to have a child, but two is a wonderful thing. Melissa answered her, stating, "I have my reasons."

As they entered the room, Officer Anderson and Mrs. Becker were sitting there, talking. She gave him some info about Melissa that he needed. Being that close to a police officer in uniform reminded her of her husband, who was also a police officer that worked night shift. She explained how worried she would be, not knowing if he would return home the next morning. After thirty years on the force, he transferred from the streets after five and retired as a detective.

"Hi, Officer. Am I in trouble for something?" asked Melissa.

"Of course not. I came by after the accident, but you were out of it. I need a statement from you about what happened," explained the officer.

"It's simple. It was raining something terrible, and I didn't see the car in front of me stop. And when I tried to stop, it was too late," explained Melissa as she gathered her things.

"I figured as much. Unfortunately, the accident will be ruled your fault since you struck the car from behind," said the officer.

"Well, that's the least of my worries. Is there anything else?" asked Melissa in frustration.

I need to see your driver's license, and the nurse will make a copy. Thank you."

"Where is my purse?" asked Melissa as she looked around frantically.

"It's in the locker. I put it there yesterday while you were sleeping," said the nurse.

The officer left, and Mrs. Becker embraced Melissa and asked, "Well?"

Melissa looked at the nurse as she started to smile with tears rolling down her face.

"I'm pregnant, Mom!" said Melissa.

"Wow, that's great! I'm so excited! And look, I don't want to be called Nana. I want to be called Grandmother," said Mrs. Becker.

They all laughed and exited the room.

On the ride home, Melissa was explaining to her mom how she was nervous about being a single parent. Her mom explained how her father's health was deteriorating fast and said that if he passed and Lonnie was not home, she would come and stay as long as needed.

"Lonnie stated he would call back tonight," stated Mrs. Becker. Mrs. Becker had assured Lonnie that Melissa was okay, and he had said he could take an emergency leave. Mrs. Becker didn't want that; she wanted to spend some time alone with Melissa, especially now that she was pregnant.

"He is going to be so happy to know he is going to be a father," said Melissa.

"He will miss the pregnancy, but I'm sure he will be able to come home on the big day," said Mrs. Becker.

Melissa was thinking otherwise. There was no way she could take care of two babies, and she had nine months to plan how to be in the delivery room alone.

*****

"Hey, honey!" said Melissa.

"What happened? Are you okay? Do you need me to come home?" asked Lonnie.

"I'm okay, just a little sore. The rain got worse, and I ran into the back of someone. Are you at your destination?"

"Yes, finally, we stopped in Germany, and it's a mess here. I can't say too much about it," explained Lonnie.

Melissa did not want to tell Lonnie about the pregnancy just yet. She was still indecisive. She was happy and afraid.

Mrs. Becker was telling Melissa about her father's condition and how it was not getting any better. If he passed, she would spend a lot of time with her to help with the baby. And she was going to need the company and support. She and Mr. Becker had been married for forty years, and it was going to be tough for Mrs. Becker to be without him after all these years.

Melissa finally told Lonnie she was pregnant but not with twins. Lonnie vowed to call three times a week to make sure his pregnant wife was okay. He promised he would be there for the birth, although there wasn't any leave that was supposed to take place until after a year.

After two days, Mrs. Becker finally left to go back home to Georgia. Melissa was alone again. She enjoyed researching names. Little by little, she bought baby clothes for a boy and girl. In her mind, she still wrestled with the fact of giving one child up. If she did, she thought, which one should she give up? And she wondered if she should tell anyone.

Before it was done or the babies were even born, it weighed heavily in her heart as each day passed. She knew she had to hurry and find a part-time job and get enrolled in school. She always wanted to be a nurse. Even though they had money in the bank and Lonnie had a decent income, she needed to stay busy.

One stormy day, while home and off from work at the local florist's, she sat in the window, crying and rubbing her stomach while watching the steady rain and anticipating the loud thunder after the flashes of lightning.

In the distance, she could see headlights creeping down the street. As the car got closer, she could see it was a police car. The turn signal flashed bright yellow as the police cruiser pulled into the driveway. The bright lights illuminated the room. Melissa backed away from the window and sat quietly, anticipating a knock at the door. It was Officer Anderson. The officer investigating the accident.

He came in and gratefully accepted the towel she offered to dry his face and hands. They exchanged pleasant greetings and sat. He stated his reason for coming by, which was to bring copies of everything and to check on her.

She accepted the documents and smiled. She apologized for being rude at the hospital. He stated he was used to being rude to.

"Is it normal for an officer to bring paperwork to someone's house and check on them?" asked Melissa.

"Well, it's an officer's discretion, and I patrol this area. It's not a problem, is it?" asked Officer Anderson.

"No, it's okay, I guess," answered Melissa.

"Okay, well, I'll go now."

"Okay, thanks for the paperwork," said Melissa. They shook hands, and he left.

The phone rang, and it was Lonnie. He had a bad day. Combat was picking up and becoming a daily duty. He wanted to be honest about what was going on but didn't want her to worry. She told him about her classes and her part-time job at the florist's shop. He asked how the baby was doing and about upcoming appointments. She told him of an appointment next week. He was excited and asked for pics of her preggo belly.

Shortly after their conversation, her mom called. Mrs. Becker wanted to tell Melissa that her father was in hospice care and that she didn't know how long he would be around. Melissa hung up the phone, packed a bag, and headed for Georgia. She wanted her father to see his grandchildren, but that was another five months away.

She arrived in Georgia, afraid of what her father might look like. She was trying not to stress out too much in fear of hurting the unborn. As she walked in the room, she immediately started to cry. Her mom embraced her to comfort her, but she had to process it in her own way. Mrs. Becker had been seeing the gradual deterioration, so the pain and emotions were manageable.

The hospice nurse stepped aside, and Mrs. Becker led Melissa to her father's side. She grabbed his hand and placed it on her stomach. He slowly opened his eyes and looked as if he didn't know who she was. She cried even harder. Melissa left the room because she couldn't stand seeing her father in that condition. She felt so helpless because she couldn't help her father. So many childhood memories flashed in her head.

Pictures of family vacations, birthday parties, and graduation lined the wall of the family room, where Melissa went to gather herself. As she sat and gazed at the pictures, she felt movement in her stomach. That came at a bad time. Seeing her father on his deathbed and then reminded she was pregnant with twins and she was the only one who knew besides the nurse but she doesn't count. She so needed her husband at this moment. There was no one to lean on or talk to.

"Melissa, come here please!" shouted her mom.

Her heart stopped in fear. She ran into the room, expecting the worse. "Yes, Mom?" she stated in fear. She then saw her father with his eyes wide opened and muttering.

When he saw her, he smiled and stretched his fingers out. Melissa hurried and rushed to his side and grabbed his hand. She leaned down and kissed him on the forehead. He squeezed her hand and began to mutter again. He definitely knew who she was.

"Daddy, you're going to be a grandfather," she said excitedly.

He smiled and raised his hand to touch her stomach. He only got a few inches away from her bulging belly and stopped because he was too weak. She then grabbed his hand, placed it on her stomach, and let go. As his hand was resting on her stomach, he looked at his wife and muttered, "Touch."

Mrs. Becker placed her hand on top of his and smiled. She stated that was the happiest she has seen him in a long time.

At that time, Mr. Becker murmured, "It's a girl."

They all laughed with excitement and joy! Melissa stayed overnight to spend time with her dad in case things took a turn for the worse. She had to get back for her doctor's appointment.

Lonnie called later that night. She told him about her dad not doing too well and said that was why she went to visit. On a better note, she explained, he touched her stomach and said it was girl. Lonnie was excited and said they needed to come up with a name for a girl. At that time, Melissa thought, *No, we're going to need two names.*

Every time Melissa talked to Lonnie, she had anxiety because she knew the subject of the baby would come up. Melissa told Lonnie about the doctor's appointment in two days. He stated he would call that day to see how it went.

*****

Lonnie called as Melissa was leaving the doctor's office.

"So how is it going with you, my soldier?" asked Melissa. There was a pause. "Hello? Honey? Are you there?" asked Melissa frantically.

"Yes, I'm here. Well, we took fire today and lost three soldiers," said Lonnie.

"OMG, honey, that's terrible. Are you okay?"

"Yea, I'm okay," said Lonnie, very sad. "I'm going to be honest, sweetheart. It's rough here, and that's the reality. This is what I signed up for, and we both knew this was a possibility," said Lonnie.

Melissa was silent and became more afraid of raising a child or two on her own.

Lonnie told her he had two scheduled leaves, one for the delivery.

Melissa sat in the car, crying and looking at the pics of the ultrasound. The two little girls growing inside her belly looked so at piece and in perfect harmony with each other. As she sat there, she thought more and more of the possibility of putting one child up for adoption, especially after the conversation with her husband. She put the pic in the glove compartment and pulled herself together as she had to go to work at the flower shop.

"Hi, Melissa," greeted the shop owner, Ms. Myra.

"Hi, how are you?" asked Melissa.

"I'm great, thanks! Look at that belly. That baby is growing. It almost looks like there are two in there," stated Myra with a chuckle.

They laughed. Melissa stated she couldn't handle that.

"Oh, someone ordered you a bouquet of red roses. They're over on the shelf. They didn't leave a name. I assume it was your husband," explained Myra.

"Oh gosh, they're beautiful," stated Melissa.

The card read, "TOY."

"What is that?" mumbled Melissa. *Probably some military term,* she thought.

*****

Melissa just finished her first semester of nursing school. She received all As and a B. With all the distractions, she had proved

14

to be mentally strong and focused. Receiving good grades gave her encouragement.

"Hi, Mom," Melissa greeted her mom on the phone.

"I'm okay," stated her mom.

There was silence, and Melissa was not thinking the worse. "I got all As and a B for my semester. I'm so happy!" said Melissa.

"Melissa, that's great. I'm so proud of you, honey. You can do anything you put your mind to. You are very intelligent and strong-willed. Don't forget that," stated her mom.

"Okay, thank you, Mom. I love you!"

"I love you too, dear."

"So how is Dad doing?" asked Melissa apprehensively.

"Melissa…your dad died last night," said her mom, weeping.

"No, NO, NO, MOM! No!" shouted Melissa, shaking. Melissa dropped the phone, crying out of control. She didn't know what to say or what to do. She had never experienced death or attended a funeral. Melissa cried herself to sleep that night.

The next day, Lonnie called to tell Melissa he was very sick. She told him her father had died. He told her he would be home as he could take a leave for a death.

Melissa got the nerves to call her mom back. Her mom told her of the arrangements. The service was in four days.

The police department where Mr. Becker retired from was very supportive. Mr. Becker would have a police-style funeral service with a twenty-one-gun salute.

*****

Lonnie's flight was delayed. Melissa picked him up from the base, and they had to go straight to Georgia. They arrived at the house, where there was a motorcade of police motorcycles and police vehicles. They hurried inside to change. Melissa started crying and couldn't stop.

It was a nice service. Mrs. Becker took it well only because she knew she was losing her husband and that it was a matter of time until he couldn't fight anymore.

Lonnie had a week for his leave, so they decided to stay for a couple of days. Once back at home in North Carolina, they hugged and kissed continually. Lonnie walked into the kitchen and saw the roses. Melissa was in the bedroom, changing. Lonnie read the card and tried to remain calm, but as soon as Melissa was done changing and walked in, he lost it. She honestly had no idea who sent them. They argued, and Lonnie accused Melissa of being unfaithful. He stormed out and went to get beer. He sat outside, on the back patio, drinking until he got drunk. He then began to argue again, this time being verbally abusive. Lonnie burst the vase and threw the flowers in the garbage. Melissa locked herself in the bedroom and cried herself to sleep.

His time was up, and they were quiet on the way to the base. Once there, he apologized. Melissa told him she no longer wanted him to drink, and he agreed. They hugged and kissed after saying their goodbyes.

Melissa went to work the next day and had a message that instructed her to call a number.

"Well, hello there."

"Hi, who is this?" asked Melissa.

"Officer Anderson, but you can call me Marcus."

"Is there something wrong?" asked Melissa.

"Yes, there is," he answered.

"What is it?" asked Melissa.

"Well, to be honest, I'm very interested in you, but you're married," he said.

"Yes, I am," she said.

"No, it's okay. I don't want to sound creepy, but you have no idea how badly I want to get to know you," explained Officer Anderson.

"Did you send flowers?" asked Melissa.

"Did you like them?" he asked.

"Yes, they were beautiful, but they caused the biggest argument between my husband and me," she said.

"I'm sorry. I don't want to cause any trouble. I thought he was overseas?" he asked.

"How do you know?" asked Melissa.

"I do my homework," he said.

"Okay, well, I have to get back to work," explained Melissa.

"Please keep my number in case you need anything. I'm here," he pleaded. "And by the way, you're pretty pregnant," he added.

*****

It was two months away from delivery, and they argued every time they spoke, especially when Lonnie was drinking. The flower thing gave Lonnie an excuse to drink more and influenced Melissa's decision to keep only one child.

*****

It was Melissa's last doctor's appointment before delivery date, and she was having twin girls. On one of the more civil phone calls, Melissa told Lonnie she was having a girl, and they both decided on the name Kristen Ivey Logan. Melissa was going to name the other girl Susanna Lee Logan.

Melissa made up her mind. She was going to keep Kristen. She discussed the adoption, and it was all ready to go, including ensuring confidentiality from everyone, including her own husband.

Melissa talked to her mom every day to make sure she was okay. Although Mrs. Becker held up in front of everyone, Melissa knew that behind closed doors, she was struggling. Melissa gave both her mom and Lonnie late delivery dates so they wouldn't be there to see both girls as she had set Susanna up for adoption.

With the date approaching, Lonnie told Melissa he would be home three days before the delivery, which was fine, according to Melissa. The babies would have already been born.

Two weeks before the delivery, Melissa ran into Officer Anderson at the hospital as she was there to sign the final adoption papers.

He hugged her and whispered, "I wish those were my babies."

She pulled away and said, "Good to see you again."

He stated it wouldn't be the last time.

As she was driving home, she remembered Officer Anderson saying "those babies." She thought how he knew she was pregnant with multiple babies.

Melissa went to work on her last day before delivery. There was a beautiful arrangement of lilies waiting for her. She called Officer Anderson to thank him and asked how he knew she liked lilies. He told her he saw her lily earrings on the day of the accident. She was flattered that he paid that much attention to her. Melissa found herself enjoying the conversation. He told her to call him after the delivery, and she agreed.

Melissa showed up two days early at the hospital because she was having contractions. Mrs. Becker called, but Melissa didn't tell her she was at the hospital because she didn't want her to come. It didn't matter because Mrs. Becker told her she was coming in the morning. Melissa told her not to come because she would be working the next two days, and Mrs. Becker agreed but was going to surprise her. Melissa became worried and wanted to hurry and deliver the babies.

In the morning, Mrs. Becker pulled in the driveway and didn't see Melissa's car. She started calling back to back. After getting no answer, she figured Melissa might have gone into labor at work, so she decided to go to the hospital.

*****

"There is number one," said the doctor.

Melissa could barely talk because of the pain and excitement. She stared and said, "That's Kristen," as she looked in disbelief at a beautiful little girl with a head full of dark hair.

The doctor already knew the second baby was Susanna, which was the baby going to adoption. Susanna came, and Melissa reached for her as she started crying. It seemed as if little Susanna opened her eyes and looked at her mother and sister as if to say, "Why can't I stay?"

Melissa cried out, "No, NO, NO! I want my baby! Please don't take her! Please!"

It was too late; they had taken her out. And besides, the papers had already been signed. As they took her out, she could hear Susanna crying as they took her down the hallway. Melissa held and kissed Kristen. Still crying and feeling guilty, she said, "Don't worry, Kristen. We will see her again."

The nurse took baby Kristen out and prepared for postdelivery. At this time, she could hear her mother's voice and thought, *Oh no.* She followed the postdelivery instructions and got herself together really fast, hoping the girls were separated. Melissa was being wheeled to recovery when she saw her mother holding Kristen. Mrs. Becker didn't see Melissa. Melissa frantically requested that her mother come to the room.

"She is so beautiful, the perfect mix of you and Lonnie," said Mrs. Becker.

"Yes, she is. I wish Dad was here to see her," said Melissa as tears rolled down her cheeks.

Lonnie called to see how Melissa was doing. He was already back on US soil, waiting to leave the next day. He was surprised and happy that the baby girl was here. He questioned Melissa, asking if she knew she would deliver the baby early. Melissa didn't want to argue in front of her mom. She told him she would see him tomorrow. As she lay there, looking at Kristen, she couldn't help but to think about the journey Susanna was about to take. She felt so guilty.

The next day, Melissa and her mom were taking pictures of Kristen and Lonnie as he held her, wearing his uniform. Melissa could smell alcohol on Lonnie and hoped they wouldn't argue while her mom was there. She had planned to stay awhile, so it was going to be a challenge unless Lonnie stopped drinking.

*****

There they sat in the car, on the base, waiting for Lonnie to leave again. There were no arguments. They were actually having a happy conversation as proud parents—a conversation prompted by the baby sitting in the back.

Lonnie had four months to go until his tour was over. They hugged and kissed, and she watched the C-130 take off again until it disappeared.

After three weeks, Mrs. Becker was packing to leave. Melissa thought the moment she feared most was at hand. As she sat there, feeding Kristen, Susanna was still on her mind. She thought that after a few weeks, she would call to see where Susanna was. While laying Kristen down, she heard a noise at the door. She opened the door, and there was a beautiful bouquet of flowers and a pink bag filled with baby items. She knew it was from Officer Anderson, so she called to thank him.

"Well, hello and thank you," said Melissa.

"You are very welcome. Please call if there is anything you need," he said.

*****

Lonnie retired from the military, and Kristen is now a teenager. They went on their first family vacation to Hawaii.

"Dad, where is the party?" asked Kristen.

"The party is actually called a luau," he answered. "And the luau will be on the beach tonight. It's going to be fun," added Lonnie.

Kristen started dancing around like the Hawaiian girls that were wearing the grass skirts. Melissa was watching her, smiling wondering where all the time had gone. Looking at Kristen, she thought if she should tell him one day.

"Honey, are you ready for your grown-up Slurpee?" Lonnie asked with an eager smile.

"Yes, let's have one," answered Melissa.

"Good. How about you come with me so you can pour your own troubles?" said Lonnie as he placed his arm around her and guided her toward the straw-covered bar. Kristen requested to remain in the sun and watched the roaring waves as surfers fought to ride the rolling waters.

*****

Kristen was sprawled out on the bed, asleep. The day on the beach drained her young body.

Melissa was standing on the balcony, taking in the view of the beautiful Hawaiian scenery. The tropical winds were lifting her hair off her shoulders. She was wearing a colorful sundress with only a thong underneath.

Lonnie stepped out of the bathroom from taking a long whiz. He came out and saw his beautiful wife standing on the balcony as if she was about to take flight. While approaching, he could see through her dress and immediately got sexually aroused. After sliding behind her, he placed one hand on her hip and slid the glass door shut with the other hand. He pulled her body against his, and she felt what he was thinking between her butt cheeks. He began to softly kiss her neck until she leaned her head back. She had accepted his seductive invitation by pressing and slowly grinding her butt against his hardness. She could feel it getting longer and harder. She grabbed his hands by his fingers, whispered his name, and pulled one hand up toward her breast and the other slowly past her navel, directly below her waist. Kissing passionately, Melissa raised herself up on her tiptoes to adjust to his hardness.

Tap, tap, tap could be heard from the glass door. Kristen was standing there. "Mom, Dad, someone is at the door."

They stopped in frustration, and Melissa went to answer the door. Meanwhile, Lonnie waited for the blood to be evenly distributed back through his body. Keeping his body turned opposite to the room, he turned his head to see who was at the door. Back in control, he stepped into the room and observed Melissa turning around with a huge fruit basket and three colorful leis.

"Who is that from mom?" asked Kristen.

"Complimentary from the hotel," answered Melissa.

Lonnie stood there, trying to look innocent, and said, "Oh, that was nice. You think they have complimentary drinks?"

"Honey, I'm sure they don't," said Melissa, not wanting him to go, afraid it might be hours before he returned. Melissa wanted to return to the balcony.

"Well, I'll just go see what the drink of the day is," said Lonnie as he started to walk toward the door.

"Honey, we can't go to the bar. Kristen is not of age," suggested Melissa.

"I know. I'll be just a minute," he pleaded.

"Dad, please don't go get drunk. I want to go to the luau tonight. You promised!" exclaimed Kristen.

"Every is going so well, honey," said Melissa as she ran over to him. She hugged him and pleaded in a soft voice, "Lonnie, please don't get drunk. This is a special vacation for us. Kristen is counting on you, and I want you to finish what you started earlier. If you drink too much, you will be abusive and pass out."

For the first time, he felt like his drinking was competing with his family. He hated feeling like this and was wondering if he really had a problem.

Melissa and Kristen had fallen asleep after talking about Lonnie's drinking problem. Kristen had vowed she would never grow up and deal with a man who drank or, for that matter, drink herself. Her mother told her that she would probably have been a sister as well as a daughter if her dad didn't have such a drinking problem. Kristen would have loved that and said she would never give up on having a sister.

There was loud talking followed by a series of knocks that awakened Melissa later that night. She got out of bed and realized it had been two hours since Lonnie left.

"Who is it?" asked Melissa.

"Honey, it's me, honey," answered a very slurred voice with heavy breathing. She peaked out the peephole and saw the very familiar drunken face of her husband along with two other men. She dreadfully opened the door and saw Lonnie being literally held up by two security officers.

"Let go of me, you jerks! This is my room, and that's my wife!" shouted Lonnie as he staggered into the room, trying to kiss Melissa.

She pushed him out the way.

"Well, fuck you too, Melissa. Fuck you!"

Kristen had awoken and ran to her mom, watching her dad toss and turn, whispering obscenities.

"Ma'am, is this your husband?" asked the older security officer.

"At the moment, unfortunately, he is. I apologize for everything," said Melissa.

"Yes, ma'am, but unfortunately, I'm going to have to ask you all to check out of the hotel."

"But why? We reserved this room for two weeks," said Melissa, frustrated.

"Because of the events caused by your husband, management has decided to revoke your stay. You can call or go down to the desk, and they will explain," explained the security officer.

"I will do just that," Melissa angrily said and slammed the door shut.

Kristen started to cry as she sat on the other bed. Her mother hugged her and assured her everything was going to be okay. Melissa turned and looked at her drunken husband in disgust as she dialed the front desk.

"Yes, this is Mrs. Logan in room 2368."

"Yes, ma'am. Hold please," said the female voice.

"Yes, honey. Who is it? Let's go to the party," Lonnie said, his speech still slurred. He was about to pass out.

"Lonnie, shut your damn mouth. I'm sick of you!" said Melissa.

"Yes, Mrs. Logan, this is Mr. Mualla, and I'm the manager of the hotel. I need to see you as soon as possible."

"Okay, I'll be right there," she said nervously. She hung up the phone and stared at Lonnie with deep frustration, wondering what was going on. She raked her fingers through her hair while looking in the mirror. She told Kristen to watch her dad while she was gone. Kristen stood and wiped her tears, begging her mother not to leave her alone with her dad.

"Kristen, I don't trust him by himself. If you need me, I'll be at the front desk. Just dial 0," instructed her mom as she walked toward the door.

"But, Mom, I'm afraid," she said as she started to tear up.

"He's passed out. I'll be right back." She closed the door and left.

Lonnie raised his head up, his eyes bloodshot. He made eye contact with Kristen's, and Kristen began to slowly walk backward toward the sofa, hoping his head would fall back to the pillow. She sat down, showing confidence, knowing her father wouldn't do anything to hurt her. But fear crept in as she observed him looking at her legs.

He rose out of the bed and looked around for his wife. "Where is your mother?"

"She went to the front desk because they said you caused trouble at the bar," explained Kristen.

He then staggered to the bathroom, where she heard him urinating and burping out of control. Kristen moved to the bed, where she could be close to the phone.

Meanwhile, at the front desk, the manager was explaining that her husband was talking very vulgarly and making obscenities at the bartender. He also stated that he attempted to go behind the bar and, in doing so, bumped into an elderly couple, knocking the woman to the ground. So as a result, it was decided that Mr. Logan was a danger to himself and others. And the very attractive native Hawaiian bartender felt threatened. So the manager had no choice but to end their stay at the very luxurious beachfront Hawaiian hotel.

Melissa didn't try to defend her husband because she knew he had a problem. After apologizing, she stood there, embarrassed but patient as charges were being refunded on the credit card.

Melissa's curiosity got the best of her. She stepped into the bar to get a look at the bartender. She looked to be barely twenty-one, she thought. She moved gracefully behind the bar with a pretty smile and a perfect body. She had dark and evenly tanned skin with silky long black hair. Her bulging breasts made it very easy for anyone to look at her. The more Melissa looked at her, the more she thought about Kristen.

The manager wasn't quite finished with the credit card, so she used the lobby phone to call the room. But there was a busy tone. As she walked back to the desk to ask if the phone had already been cut off, she thought that maybe she might not have hung it up after the earlier call.

*****

Lonnie came out of the bathroom and noticed that Melissa had still not returned.

"Dad, please stop. I don't want a hug," begged Kristen.

During a small struggle, he knocked the phone over. He was forcibly trying to hug her, and she was resisting. They fell to the bed. The strong smell of alcohol scared her, and his drunken strength caused her to almost scream. Lonnie was known to become very intimate when he was drunk. Sitting on the bed, he hugged her tight, telling her how much he loved her. Kristen began to cry while not resisting anymore, hoping her mom would walk in and rescue her. He loosened his clutch and rubbed her head, his other hand resting on her leg.

Melissa stormed through the door. "Get your fucking hands off her," she said angrily while she pushed him in the face. Kristen ran to the couch, put her head in her lap, and started to cry.

Her mother kneeled down beside her to console her. "What did he do to you?"

She rose up and hugged her mom tightly.

"Honey, what's wrong with her?" mumbled Lonnie as he attempted to stand.

"Shut your fucking mouth, you son of a bitch. We have to leave! I can't believe you would go down there and cause a scene like that. Kristen and I are leaving, going back home. You can stay if you want, but you will go to jail. I hate you, Lonnie. If you don't get help, I promise you will never see us again."

"Shut your damn mouth right now, Melissa," he slurred as he stood up, holding on to the lamp.

She walked over to him, stuck her finger in his face, and stated, "We are leaving in ten minutes with or without you."

He pushed her onto the bed and started falling on top of her. Immediately she scooted back and kicked him to the floor.

"Kristen, go to the door," she said hurriedly.

While he was trying to stand, Melissa was looking for the phone. She saw it on the floor, partially under the bed. She attempted to reach for it when he gained his footing. He pulled her hair, and she elbowed him in the midsection. He threw up and fell back to the floor. Melissa grabbed the phone to call for help, but it had already been disconnected.

Kristen, already terrified, screamed as the door flung open, and in came the police. Melissa crawled over to Kristen and hugged her in relief. The police had already been made aware of Lonnie and the problems he had caused. Additional officers arrived and handcuffed him.

"Are you okay, ma'am?" asked the plump officer.

"Yes, we're fine. He is really drunk and got out of hand. We're preparing to go back to the US," she stated.

"I'm afraid he won't be going back, at least for another twenty-four hours. He is to remain in custody until he sobers up," explained Corporal Dole. She looked at Kristen as she looked at her dad with fear and anger.

Surely, I can't leave him in Hawaii, she thought as the officers struggled to get him up.

Corporal Dole gave her the number and address to the jail.

"Thank you, and I'm sorry for all of the trouble," says Melissa as they carried him out the door.

Lonnie could barely walk and struggled to talk, asking for forgiveness. Mr. Mualla appeared and offered to extend their stay another night since Mr. Logan wasn't going to be there. Before any thought, she agreed but requested another room. It was no problem.

*****

Melissa and Kristen made their way to the luau and were having a good time. They sat and sampled different native lemonades.

"Mom, let's go try it!" asked Kristen excitedly, pointing to the tourists who were wearing the traditional grass skirts.

"Come on, Mom. They're about to show them how to hula." Kristen stood up and pulled her mom up.

Two of the native women came over and asked them to join in. Before they made their way to the crowd, they fixed them with grass skirts and placed leis around their necks. They were dancing and having a good time. The events that happened earlier didn't stop them from enjoying the vacation.

During the fun, Melissa glanced over and saw the same woman who was the victim of Lonnie's earlier harassment. She wanted to make her way over to her but didn't know if she should.

Kristen found a dance partner: a little girl that looked to be around the same age.

Now is the perfect time to go over and investigate, Melissa thought.

The woman disappeared into a crowd of workers who were preparing food and drinks.

"Honey, I'm going to go have a seat. You're doing well!" said Melissa with a big smile. Melissa made it back to their table and sat while looking around for the lady.

The lady walked by with a plate of exotic fruit—a dish that was a tradition at luaus.

"Excuse me," the lady said. "Do you know if this table is taken?"

"I believe it is, but you can sit with me," answered Melissa.

"Are you here alone?" asked the woman as she was sitting down.

"No, my daughter and I here alone on vacation," explained Melissa warmly.

"Where is your husband?" asked the lady.

"How do you know I'm married?" asked Melissa, surprised.

"I see you have a ring on," stated the woman.

"I was engaged, but unfortunately, it was called off. But I kept the ring."

"Would you like some fruit?" asked the lady.

"Sure," answered Melissa. They talked a little and got acquainted. The woman gave Melissa good tourist information and told her about Hawaiian history. Melissa was thinking of how to mention the problem she had earlier. She didn't want to seem nosy or probing.

"Excuse me, Lola. You forgot to sign your time sheet," a man informed the woman. He looked to be some kind of waiter. They both had the same kind of shirt on. She signed the paper, and he left.

"Do you work here?" asked Melissa.

"Well, actually, I work at the hotel's bar and restaurant. I sometimes do parties like these for additional income. Like yourself, it's just me and my daughter," explained the woman.

This is my chance, thought Melissa. "Were you at the bar earlier today when some drunk was causing an awful scene?"

The woman touched her hand and said, "OMG, yes! I was working at the bar. After about three drinks, he began telling me how good he could make me feel. He said that he was here on vacation alone."

That son of a bitch, thought Melissa.

"He also said he retired from the military just recently. And to top it off, he tried to come behind the bar. Lord knows what he would have done. The security saw the whole thing and rescued me," she explained.

"Hey, Mom, meet my new friend, Susanna," Kristen excitedly said.

"Mom, this is my new friend, Kristen," said the other little girl. Both daughters had paired up as well as the mothers. What a coincidence. They were all formally introduced.

Chills rushed all over Melissa's body as she stared at Susanna. *My god,* she thought, *they look so much alike.* No one else could see what she saw because no one else knew what she knew.

"Susanna, you are a pretty little girl. How old are you?" asked Melissa.

"I'm fourteen," answered the girl in a sweet voice as she hugged her mom.

"I'm fourteen too," said Kristen joyfully.

"When is your birthday?" asked Kristen.

Melissa then intentionally knocked over her drink as she didn't want to know the answer to that question.

She thought she had better get to know Lola and Susanna better. If Susanna was who she thought she was, she would feel a lot better, knowing where she was.

The girls got along so well together. They acted as if they knew each other before they met. Perhaps they did in an earlier lifetime, she imagined. Dismissing the possibilities, she knew it could never happen like this. After Melissa cleaned up the mess, she mentioned it was getting late and said she and Kristen had a flight to catch in the morning.

"Mom, I want to see Susanna before we leave."

"Yea, can they come visit tomorrow, Ma?" asked Susanna as she stood between Kristen and Melissa, holding Kristen's hand.

Before Lola could answer, Melissa insisted that they take a picture of the three of them holding hands. The camera clicked. Melissa couldn't wait to get the film developed. She almost wanted to get it done before the left the island.

"Sure, I'm off tomorrow. Maybe we could give you guys a ride to the airport," suggested Lola.

"That sounds good," agreed Melissa.

The girls hugged each other with joy. Lola gave Melissa the telephone number and told her to call when they're ready.

"Mom, what about Dad?" asked Kristen, not knowing she wasn't supposed to mention a third party. Melissa hugged Kristen to sort of play it off and prayed Lola didn't hear that. They said their goodbyes and parted.

The next morning, Melissa had awoken before Kristen. As they lay there in bed, the first thing she saw was the camera and the paper with Lola's number on it. She began to daydream back to that morning in the delivery room. She tried not to look at the babies after birth because she knew she would never see one of them again. At least that was what she thought.

"Mom, what time is it?" asked Kristen in her morning voice.

"It's time to get up, honey. We have to pack and check out."

"Am I still going to see Susanna?" asked Kristen.

"Yes, honey, you'll see her before we leave," said her mom. "You really like her, huh?" asked Melissa.

"Yes, I wish I had a sister like her or even a best friend. You think maybe she can come visit us in North Carolina?"

"I don't know. That's something we would have to work on."

Melissa later called the jail to see what time Lonnie could be released. They advised her that he had been released over an hour ago. She had to hurry and call Lola to get picked up. She didn't want to see him until they were back in the US. And more importantly, she wanted Kristen to see Susanna again. And she wanted to see her as well.

Melissa called Lola and told her they were ready and that she could pick them up at the gift shop next door. She didn't want to take a chance and run into Lonnie.

While checking out, she left their flight information at the desk for Lonnie. Surely, he would take a taxi to the airport and fly back to North Carolina if he found out that they had already gone, she thought. Melissa instructed Kristen not to say anything about her dad to Susanna.

"Are we all set?" asked Lola as they crammed inside a small compact car bound for the airport.

"I hate that we have to leave so soon, being that we just met," stated Melissa.

"Yea, I know. We had a good time, though. And Susanna talked about Kristen all night. Do you have any more children?"

"No, I don't," answered Melissa as she looked out the window. "How about you? Does Susanna have any brothers or sisters?" asked Melissa.

"That's something I'll explain to you later," she answered. It was as if there was a secret story behind Susanna, and she didn't want Susanna to know about it.

When they all arrived at the airport, Susanna and Kristen hugged and shed tears. They had become so close in a short amount of time. They exchanged numbers, and Kristen promised she would call once they got home. Melissa expressed her gratitude for the ride and all the hospitality. Susanna gave Kristen her favorite teddy bear, her sleeping companion since birth. They expressed their goodbyes and agreed to all keep in touch.

Thirty thousand feet in the air, somewhere between Hawaii and North Carolina, Melissa and Kristen sat in a Delta 747, flying the friendly skies. Kristen was reclined back in a window seat, sleeping. She was cuddling her new teddy bear, which she named Susie after Susanna. Her mom was looking at the aisles, watching the stewardesses take orders from passengers. She was not really excited about seeing her husband. She hoped he wouldn't arrive home before her and Kristen.

Fifteen years of marriage, and this was the first time they went on vacation together and returned separated. Melissa knew that Lonnie's alcoholism was progressing and thought that now that he was retired, the drinking would progress, which could put the family in jeopardy. She really loved him and would do what it took to help him. She grew up in a household with an alcoholic father and saw the tough times her mother had endured. She would support him only if he got help. They hadn't really talked about his future plans but knew they couldn't make it on her salary as a nurse.

A bit of turbulence caused Kristen to change her position. Li'l Susie, the teddy bear, fell out of Kristen's grasp an onto Melissa's lap. Melissa carefully picked up Susie so as not to awaken Kristen. She looked at it and smelled it. She then began to pet it and noticed a small tag around its neck that read, "I belong to Susanna Ramulla, born March 10, 1992."

OMG, she thought. She looked at Kristen, then stared out the window. But she was looking at a mental picture of Susanna. Her heart began to beat fast, and her hands sweated profusely.

Kristen awoke. "Mom, I have to go to the bathroom."

Melissa quickly placed the bear between them and sat up so Kristen could get through to the restroom. After ripping the tag off, she didn't know what to do with it but felt like she had to do something with it before Kristen returned. Quickly she folded it once and stuck it in her bra.

"Mom, how much longer do we have to go?" asked Kristen as she returned.

"A few more hours, sweetheart. Are you hungry?"

"Yes, a little," she answered as she placed the bear in her lap.

"Do you think Li'l Susie is hungry?" asked her mom.

Kristen looked up at her with a smile, and they both giggled.

Melissa stopped one of the busy stewards and asked for two sandwiches and water. While waiting for their snacks, Kristen asked where Susie was. Her mom pulled the bear out and handed it to her gently as if it was a real baby. After they finished their sandwiches, the pilot gave an estimated landing time of thirty minutes and the weather conditions of the destination. They both were happy that they were almost home. Melissa was a bit apprehensive because she knew Lonnie, either sober or drunk, was going to be pissed because they didn't come back together. And she knew he would blame going to jail on her.

*****

Kristen got permission to call Susanna. While they were talking, her parents were arguing over the fact that the vacation was a total wreck as Melissa blamed it all on his drinking. As Kristen got older, she had begun to hate her dad for drinking so much. She knew that if she told her mom about what happened in Hawaii, she would be very upset. But she also didn't want it to happen again. As a result of all that, she was afraid to be around him, especially when he was drinking.

After a few days had passed, all was back to normal. Lonnie had agreed to get some help. He had agreed in the past but failed to follow through.

"Getting help is the only guarantee that will save our family and your life," said Melissa.

"I know, honey, and there is nothing more that I want than my family," said Lonnie.

"I'll even research AA meetings and self-help groups," offered Melissa.

"Okay," he agreed. "But promise you will go with me?" he asked.

"Sure, I'm going to stand by you all the way," she promised while grabbing his hand.

Melissa made up her mind that this was the last chance she would give him. She no longer wanted to be married to an alcoholic. And she didn't want Kristen hating her father for the rest of her life.

Melissa had an all-new task: researching the life of Susanna. She was afraid of what she might find but knew she had to know. First, she would call the Department of Vital Statistics to see if she could get any adoption information. She was nervous. She knew she had to be discreet and wasn't good at sneaking around. There could be no risk in any returned calls or mail received.

"Honey, our first meeting is tomorrow at 7:00 p.m.," said Melissa.

"Good. You know, Melissa, I'm looking forward to going."

"I think you should explain to Kristen that you are trying to get help."

"Yea, you're right. I don't know how, but I'll do my best," said Lonnie.

"Just be honest and genuine. She will understand. After dinner tonight would be a good time, I think," suggested Melissa.

"Yes, I think so," agreed Lonnie as Melissa gave him a hug.

He was thinking all along that he might need a drink to help him explain. He planned to sneak into his private stock while Melissa was cooking. Little did he know that Melissa knew about his private stock and had gotten rid of it. There was no alcohol in the house. She had even gave the cooking wines to the neighbors.

Dinner was over, and Melissa had started to clean up. Lonnie told Kristen he needed to talk to her. Kristen gazed at her mom and then back at him. He explained that it was very important.

"Okay, I'm listening," said Kristen.

"No, honey, let's go out back so your mom can finish the dishes."

"Go ahead, sweetheart," stated Melissa.

It was a nice breezy spring evening. The sun was setting, and darkness would be approaching. Out back was a gazebo and a light in the corner of the yard. Only their shadows could be seen from the house.

"Kristen, I want to apologize for my obsessive drinking. I don't want you to grow up hating me," explained Lonnie.

"I don't hate you, Dad. I'm just afraid of you when you're drunk," said Kristen.

"I know, and it shouldn't be like that. I need to control my drinking and not let it control me. As a result of all of this, I'm going to get help," said Lonnie.

"What kind of help, Dad?" she asked.

"Well, there is this group of people who share the same problem, and it's called Alcoholics Anonymous," explained Lonnie.

"Where do they meet, and what do they talk about?" she asked, curious.

"This particular group meets at the civic hall in town. And to be honest with you, I don't know what to expect," he explained.

"Are you afraid, Dad?"

"The only thing I'm afraid of is not getting better and losing my family," he said.

Kristen leaned over and hugged her dad.

*****

In a room of about twenty people consisting of men and women sat Lonnie and Melissa. There were all types of races and people of different ages, both young and old. After some reading was done, it was asked that all first-timers attending please stand. Melissa nudged Lonnie. He stood along with two other males and a female. The first two guys introduced themselves first, and then Lonnie did. He sat down, and Melissa patted him on the leg with a wink. After only thirty minutes into the meeting, he felt above those people. He didn't think of himself as a street drunk or someone who was totally dependent on alcohol. As they sat there, he grew restless, and his mind wandered to other places. At times, he could feel Melissa looking at him. Maybe she was trying to gauge his interest level. He knew it, so he would pretend to be tuned in. He thought then that he was only pleasing her and not fulfilling the purpose. They talked a lot about being honest, and he knew that was the one thing he couldn't be this early. The forefront person of the meeting started soliciting personal experiences from other attendees.

"Is there anyone who would like to share a story or experience?"

After a few moments of silence and everyone looking around at one another, a Black man in a wheelchair was pushed to the front by who appeared to be his wife.

"Yes, I would. My name is Frank, and I'm an alcoholic."

"Hi, Frank," everyone greeted.

"I haven't touched a drink in two years, and it really feels good. I started drinking when I was twelve years old. And I guess I was an alcoholic by the age of fifteen. I dropped out of school and went to live with my grandparents. My grandfather died when I was eighteen, and my grandmother a year later. My drinking went to a whole new level. I started stealing to get money to support my drinking. I went to jail a few times and prison once, all due to drinking. In my late twenties, I got married and had two daughters.

"Somehow I was able to hide my drinking until my thirty-third birthday. I got really drunk and abusive toward my wife. My daughters saw it and were devastated. I was out of control.

"I lost my family, my job, and everything I worked for. At that point, I didn't want to live anymore. I sat under a bridge, drinking a fifth of Gilbey's Gin, watching the cars and semis pass by at high speeds. And I thought…all I had to do was walk into that traffic, and it would be all done with. I finished the bottle and began to cry. I could never live a normal life, my daughters were fatherless, and my wife hated me. I got up and staggered to the flow of traffic. As I got to the bottom of the embankment, I stepped on a bottle and fell into the oncoming traffic. A truck traveling at seventy miles per hour ran over me at my waist. As you can see, I'm in a wheelchair. It's because I'm paralyzed. I will never walk again."

The man paused for a moment as he started to tear up. The lady standing behind him rubbed his shoulders. Someone else gave him tissue. The sympathy and sorrow were so thick in the room.

Lonnie looked at Melissa. She couldn't fight her tears any longer. He put his arm around Melissa as he felt so bad for the guy.

After gathering himself, the man continued. "The news covered the accident, and my wife happened to be watching. She came to the hospital and has been there since that day and every step of the way.

That was two years ago. Today I can say I have my family back with a grandson and a granddaughter. Even though it's been two years ago, I can't stop coming to these meetings. They are saving my life. If I ever take another drink, I may not be so lucky. The lady you see standing behind me is my angel, and I call her my wife. Thank you."

The story was an eye-opener and also a lesson to be learned. Lonnie had a much different outlook. Before they left, everyone greeted and introduced themselves. Some even exchanged phone numbers to keep one another lifted up until the next meeting.

On the way home, Melissa could sense the emotion that Lonnie was caught up in. She didn't know what to say. It appeared he might be a little afraid. He didn't realize the seriousness of his drinking.

"I didn't know that alcoholism was a disease," said Lonnie.

"I didn't either, and it can be inherited from parents," stated Melissa.

"Hopefully this book will educate me a little more. I'll be honest with you, Melissa. I don't know if I can go the rest of my life without a drink."

*****

"Kristen Ivey!" Melissa shouted toward Kristen's room.

"Yes, Mom? What is it?"

"The phone bill is six hundred dollars, all due to calls to Hawaii."

"I'm sorry, Mom. I didn't realize—"

"Well, you're going to help pay for this, and that means no allowance for a month. Don't make another call. I mean it," Melissa angrily stated.

Kristen stormed to her room, crying. She was trying to bear the thought of not being able to talk to Susanna. With only a couple of months left in the school year, she dreamed of spending the summer in Hawaii with Susanna. If her parents wouldn't permit her to go, she would run away. After all, her father was an alcoholic, and her mother was overly stressed.

One night, Melissa and Kristen had started eating dinner without Lonnie. He had called and said he would be late because of business he had to take care of on the base. Melissa figured he was telling the truth, but he had met with some of his military buddies to have drinks. She hoped that wasn't the case.

After dinner, they were cleaning up. Kristen assured her mom that she would help with the phone bill and not make that mistake again. This was only because of the plan she had.

Lonnie came home hours later after Melissa and Kristen had gone to bed. He staggered to the bedroom and flipped the light on.

"Honey, I'm home," he said with bloodshot eyes and a goofy grin.

Awakened out of her sleep, Kristen looked at him and knew he had been drinking. He reeked of alcohol and looked awful.

"I can't believe that after going to that meeting, you would go out and get drunk. Don't you care about us and your life?"

"Yes, I do, and I care about you," he said as he started taking off his clothes.

He was looking at Kristen's perfectly sized breasts and could see her brown nipples through her nightgown. When she sat up in bed, her gown rose up, and he got a glance of her neatly trimmed pubic triangle. She realized his thoughts and covered herself. After getting down to his boxers, he approached her. She started screaming and calling out to her mom.

"Mom! Mom, he's going to hurt me! Help! Help!" she screamed.

Melissa turned over but didn't awaken. She heard her daughter screaming but figured she was dreaming.

"Shhh, Daddy wants to talk to you, sweetheart."

"No! No, get away! Mom, help me please!" she yelled at the top of her voice.

He staggered toward the bed and lunged at her. She stood up in the bed, and he missed her. She was now standing in the corner, crying and terrified, wondering why her mother hadn't come to rescue her. As he sat on the bed with his hand stretched out, asking her to come to him, she could see his hardness protruding against his boxers. She cried out even louder and screamed as hard as she could. She screamed so hard she began to cough.

At this time, he crawled up in front of her and tugged on her leg behind her thigh, just below her buttocks. She lost her footing on the sheets and slipped. She fell on her back in the bed. Her nightgown scrunched up just above her navel. Because she slept pantyless, she was exposed. She saw his eyes gaze at her vagina. As he began to lower his head, she crossed her legs tightly and began to scream again.

Melissa appeared in the doorway. Terrified and angry at what she saw, she yelled at him to stop. His head then fell between her legs. Melissa grabbed a golf club and hit him as hard as she could at the back of the head. Blood gushed out everywhere while he held his head. She dropped the club and reached over to grab Kristen. He rose up, wailing in pain, and backhanded her across the room. She fell on the floor, and he stood up and started yelling obscenities. He reached down and grabbed her by the hair. Kristen got up, picked up the golf club, and struck him in the same spot her mother had hit. He collapsed to the floor, motionless. They both ran to the spare bedroom and locked the door. Huddled in the closet, they cried and hugged each other.

"Honey, are you okay?" asked her mom.

"Yea," she answered in a whisper, still crying.

She wanted to call the police, but there was no phone in the spare bedroom. Kristen was begging to leave. She never wanted to see her father again.

They left and checked into a hotel for the night. Melissa knew that was it. She was going to file for divorce. She wanted so badly to know what happened but was afraid to ask. Kristen couldn't sleep; she was terrified. Melissa knew that she would never allow him to see her again. Her plans were to go back to the house the following day and pack, and then they'd go on to her parents' house in Georgia.

On approaching the house, they could see an ambulance, and the streets were filled with police cars. She wanted to stop until she saw the yellow police tape around the front of the house. She got really nervous. Her heart started to beat out of control. Hurriedly she drove off the street so she wouldn't be noticed by the neighbors. She thought about calling Officer Anderson but was afraid.

"Mom, what's wrong? Why didn't you stop?" asked Kristen.

She didn't answer. She focused on the road and continued to look in the rearview mirror to make sure they weren't being followed. She gripped the steering wheel tightly and drove like a robot.

"Mom, what do you think happened?" Kristen asked frantically.

"I don't know, but I think we hurt him badly," she answered.

"He deserved it," said Kristen.

From that statement, Melissa knew that if they had killed him, Kristen would stand by her. *What if he is dead?* she thought. They would be charged with murder. An autopsy would show blunt force trauma to his head. And the weapon was still there with both of their fingerprints on it.

*****

Susanna had graduated high school and was applying for college. After being accepted to several universities, she decided to attend the University of Virginia, but that was only because she would be close to Kristen. To complete the enrolment process, the university required her to submit a high school transcript, SAT scores, and a birth certificate. She had everything except her birth certificate. Her mom knew if she gave her the birth certificate, she would question the names. Although Lola made a promise to herself that when Susanna reached eighteen years old, she would explain everything to her. After giving it some thought, Lola became reluctant. She didn't want her to go to college with uncertainty about who she was, but she still was apprehensive.

"If you will give me everything you need to send off, I'll mail it on the way to work," said Lola.

"Okay, Mom. Thanks."

"I'm so proud of you, Susanna. You've been wonderful over the years. I know you will do well in college and live a successful life," her mom said as she stroked her silky black hair.

"And you are the best mom in the world!" she exclaimed, hugging her mom.

Susanna tried repeatedly to call Kristen but couldn't get an answer. She wanted to give her the good news that she would be going to college only three hours away from her.

She received her official acceptance letter and the date for her freshman orientation. She and her mom both decided that she would leave early and take a few summer courses. She also wanted to work to buy a car. She had already planned to drive to see Kristen. But she had no idea of the turmoil that lay ahead for her.

Kristen wanted to call Susanna to inform her of her move to Georgia. But because of the way they left, she left her number at home. Melissa decided to drive to Georgia. She figured it would look suspicious if they caught a plane out of town the day after the incident.

After crossing the Georgia line, she started taking back roads in case there was a lookout in Georgia since that was where her parents had lived. She could see police lights up ahead illuminating the dark road she was on as she got closer. Kristen was asleep, and she started to panic. As she got closer, she could see it was a roadblock. All she could think about was her and her daughter going to jail for murder.

"Hello, ma'am," greeted the officer as he and several other officers shined their flashlights in the car.

"Hi. What's going on, officer?" asked Melissa in fear.

"We've had a child abduction," he answered sternly.

"Okay. My daughter and I are headed to my mother's house," explained Melissa, shaking like a leaf.

"Why are you so nervous, ma'am? Please you and your daughter step out of the car please."

Melissa shook Kristen awake and told her to step out of the car. Kristen woke up, saw the officers and lights, and started crying in fear.

"Mom? Mom, what's wrong? Do they know?" she asked.

"No, honey." Melissa hugged her close and shushed her, praying the police didn't hear her.

The officers looked in the trunk and searched the car. After a few questions, they released them back on their way.

*****

"Well, hello there. What a surprise!" said Mrs. Becker.

"Hey, Mom," Melissa greeted her mom.

"And hello there, little lady," said Kristen's grandmother as she hugged her.

"Hey, Grandma," Kristen shyly said.

"Where is Lonnie?" asked Melissa's mom.

Melissa stood behind Kristen with her hands on Kristen's shoulders. She gazed at the floor and took a deep breath. She lifted her head with a serious look as her eyes filled with tears.

"My god, what's wrong, Melissa?" asked her mom as she took her hand and led her to the kitchen table.

"Something terrible has happened," Melissa said, looking into her mother's eyes.

"What is it, sweetheart? Talk to me," she demanded.

"Lonnie came in drunk and tried to rape Kristen." Before she could finish, she started crying.

"Are you sure?"

She then explained what she saw that night and described how terrified Kristen was.

"What did you do? Did you call the police? Is she hurt?"

"I wanted to get him off her, so I hit him in the head with a golf club. He then tried to attack me, so she hit him again. He fell to the floor, bleeding badly, and didn't move," explained Melissa.

"OMG, how bad is he hurt?"

"I don't know. We stayed in a hotel last night. We were going back this morning, but I didn't stop."

"Why not?" asked her mom.

"There were cops everywhere and an ambulance. They had put yellow tape around the front of the house. You know the kind you see on TV when someone has been killed," she said nervously.

"Somehow we have to find out. I'm sure the police want to talk to you," stated her mom.

"I wish Dad was here, and what if we accidentally did—"

Mrs. Becker stopped Melissa before she could finish, then sat beside her. "Whatever the case might be, you did what you thought was right at the time."

"I'm so afraid, Mom," said Melissa.

"I know, sweetheart. We'll pray about it. How about you guys get some sleep, and we will start fresh tomorrow?"

"Okay," Melissa whispered, giving her mom a hug.

*****

Susanna had finished the summer quarter and bought a nice used car. She tried to call Kristen several times but still got no answer. She called the directory and asked if they would cross-reference the number and give her an address.

Now she had an address and was going to drive to North Carolina. Hours later, she pulled into the driveway of the address she had been given. The house looked empty, she thought. There was one car in the driveway. She knocked on the door and rang the doorbell, but no answer came. Thinking she might have the wrong house, she looked in the mailbox to see if there was mail with a name on it. There were several advertisements and a letter from the state of North Carolina Department of Vital Statistics. It was addressed to Mrs. Melissa Nicole Logan and Ms. Susanna Lee Logan. She wondered why her name along with Kristen's mom's name would be on the same piece of paper. She wanted to open it but knew she wasn't supposed to. After looking to make sure no one was watching her, she took the letter and left. She found her way to the beach and decided to park there and read the letter.

Dear Mrs. Logan,

The information you requested is as follows: Susanna Lee Logan, born March 10, 1992, at 9:33 a.m. to mother Melissa Nicole Logan and father Lonnie Craig Logan at UNC Health Rex Hospital. Susanna Logan was adopted by Lola Ramulla on March 11, 1992, by permission of the paternal mother and the state of North Carolina.

She started crying, not believing what she just read. She wanted to call her mom to ask why she hadn't told her the truth over the years. She didn't know whether to be angry or happy to know the truth. After reading the letter over several times, it sunk in. *How would I get to know another mom?* she thought. The only thing that softened the blow was Kristen being her sister. She wanted to tell Kristen before anyone else. But she wondered if Kristen already knew. Surely, she thought enough of her to tell her, she wondered. Her mind raced with all sorts of thoughts as she drove back over to the Logans' residence. The same car was in the driveway, and nothing else had seemed to change. After ringing the doorbell several times, she decided to walk around to the back.

A neighbor was advised by detectives to call and report any activity around the Logans' house, and within minutes several police patrol cars and detectives surrounded the house, their guns drawn. They met Susanna at the back of the house.

"Freeze! Freeze! Get your hands up now!"

"What have I done?" she pleaded, crying in fear.

They handcuffed her and read her Miranda rights. She was crying and yelling hysterically. She thought she was being set up. They wouldn't tell her anything. They asked her name and compared her to a picture they had. From looking at the picture, they knew they had a suspect.

At the homicide station, they explained to her what was going on and why she was being arrested. She was so helpless in a place where she didn't know anyone. She explained that her sister and mother lived there and that she was only coming to visit. She also told them about the adoption letter that she had left in her car. But they refused to believe her. They insisted she was Kristen trying to bear false identification.

After repeatedly telling them she knew nothing about the events that had taken place, she was booked on second-degree murder with a two-hundred-thousand-dollar bond. She declined a phone call and sat in a cell alone, still not believing all of this was happening.

The next day, a court-appointed attorney came to visit her. She explained that she was from Hawaii and was attending the University of Virginia. She met Kristen and Melissa in Hawaii while they were vacationing. Wanting to surprise Kristen, she drove down to visit. Thinking she might have the wrong address, she looked in the mailbox for a name. That was when she discovered that Melissa was her mother and Kristen was her sister.

It all sounded like a fairy tale, the attorney thought, but he was willing to take the case and assured her everything would be okay.

"Do you think you can make a bond?" he asked.

"How much is it?"

"Two hundred thousand, which you would need 10 percent of."

"No way, I don't have that much money," she said as she began to cry.

"Have you spoken with anyone since you've been here?"

"No, I don't want to call my mom yet. My mother's in Hawaii."

"Take my card and call me if you need anything. In the meantime, I'm going to look into the adoption thing."

"Please help me, and thank you," she pleaded. She took the card and laid it on the little desk. After a sleepless night, she was going to try to lie down and rest. She said a silent prayer and drifted off to sleep.

*****

The news of Lonnie Logan's murder and his daughter taken into custody as a suspect hit the media. Melissa saw it in a news flash on TV. Her mother had taken Kristen to the supermarket. She couldn't believe he was dead. But the craziest thing was having his daughter in custody. She didn't know what to do. *Should I call the police station to see who the suspect is?* she thought. What would her mom think? Would she make her turn herself in? What would Kristen think about Susanna being her sister? Would she try to save her by telling her the truth? All these were going through Melissa's head. She didn't want them to know just yet until she came up with something. She would suggest they go out to eat after they returned home so they couldn't watch the TV.

*****

They were all enjoying their meals at Mrs. Becker's favorite steak house. Melissa could sense her mother wanted to bring up Lonnie.

"Melissa, hon, have you tried to check on your husband?"

"No, Mom, but I will do it first thing in the morning. I'll call the house to see if he is there. If not, I'll call the hospital," she replied.

They all lowered their gazes. Kristen continued to eat. It seemed as if she didn't care either way.

Melissa was worried about the story being in the Sunday paper. She knew her mother got the paper delivered early every Sunday morning. *Should I take the chance and let her find out? Maybe she will have sympathy or tell the truth about everything.* In the back of her mind, she knew that somehow the truth had to be told. The thought of her and Kristen going to prison even crossed her mind.

The next day, she called the police department, pretending to be a reporter seeking information on the suspect in the Logan murder. They told her the suspect was a daughter of the Logan family but stated she was adopted at birth and lived in Hawaii and was now attending college in Virginia. That was all the information they were willing to give.

OMG, she thought, *it's Susanna. How does she know where we lived? And what bad timing. Not to mention she knows she had been adopted.* The pressure was really on for the truth to be told, and Melissa knew everything. She could not let her be accused of this but didn't want to face it herself. There wasn't much time left. *What would I tell Mom when she asks if I've checked on Lonnie?* she thought.

The next day, surprisingly, she got up early after not getting much sleep. She and her mom prepared Saturday breakfast: pancakes made from scratch, scrambled eggs, ham, toast, and freshly squeezed orange juice. She remembered eating the same breakfast when she was growing up.

"You know, I just don't feel right about this whole situation," said Melissa's mom

"I'm sure he will be okay, but I don't know if our marriage will continue," said Melissa.

"No, I mean it's something else," said her mom, gazing at her suspiciously.

"It will all work out, Mom. This isn't anything that hasn't happened to any other couple before."

Her mom told her to sit down. They both sat at the breakfast table, across from each other. Her mom held both of her hands. A few seconds of silence passed. Melissa looked at the floor through the glass table, and her mom was gazing at her. She was feeling as though her mom was giving her a chance to tell her something. Silence continued to grow as she squeezed her hands. She slowly lifted her head and had tears in her eyes, displaying an uncertain countenance.

"Honey, Lonnie is dead," said her mom as she placed her hands on the side of her cheeks and started to cry.

"Mom, how do you know?" she asked as she walked around to hug her.

"I called to see what was going on because I didn't believe you. This is a serious matter, Melissa. You need to go back there and tell the police what happened."

"I was only protecting my daughter. I didn't mean to—"

"I have retained an attorney for you," said her mom.

"I'm so afraid, Mom. What if they try to put me in jail?"

"The attorney will handle all of that."

Obviously she didn't know about Susanna being held as a suspect. Surely, she would have mentioned it Melissa thought. It was still unclear how Susanna was apprehended.

*****

Susanna's attorney went to visit her with bad news. He couldn't find any records of adoption on his client's behalf. She assured him that the birth and adoption had taken place in North Carolina. The papers Susanna read clearly stated that. The papers were still in Susanna's car, which was being held as evidence. He suggested she call her mom in Hawaii. She should have records of the adoption. He also got her signature to get her first-quarter transcript to prove she was in school at the time of the incident.

"Can I give you my number in Hawaii to call my mom?"

"Yes, that will be fine," he answered.

He wrote the number down. He assured her that he would call as soon as he could. The adoption papers and school transcript were the two pieces of evidence that could free her, other than Kristen and Melissa coming forward with the truth. The trial was set to begin in a week.

Mr. Hartley, Susanna's attorney, tried calling Lola every day but got no answer. It was because she had decided to surprise Susanna at school. She had been there for two days but couldn't find her on the huge campus. She had no idea Susanna was about to be tried for murder.

Mr. Hartley went to see Susanna again, this time with good news. The detectives had evidence that could free her but weren't going to disclose it until the trial. He did advise her that he had a copy of the autopsy report. It indicated that the victim had an alcohol level of 0.3.

"How are you?" Mr. Hartley said.

"I'm alive," she answered

"I've been trying to reach your mom in Hawaii."

"OMG, where is she? You think she may—"

"I'll keep trying. Do you want me to leave a message?" he asked.

"Yes, please. I'm getting desperate. Still no luck on Kristen and Melissa?" asked Susanna.

"No, detectives are searching for them. I mean searching for Melissa because they think you are Kristen."

"I don't know what to do. I'm innocent. I have no idea what went on in that house," she said desperately.

"I'm going to do everything I can to prove that. Trial starts Monday. I'll be back on Friday or sooner if I find out anything. Don't worry. It will all work out," he said with confidence.

Susanna didn't think Kristen and Melissa would let her take the blame for this if they knew about it. They both knew that she had never seen Mr. Logan before. She thought she was being framed, but why and by who? She would continue to hide the fact that she was adopted if that was what they wanted. She knew she would go free. Justice had to be served. The record of the adoption was all she needed. *But then where would that leave Kristen if they think I'm her?* she thought. Maybe the reason Mr. Hartley couldn't reach Lola was that perhaps she got word of everything that was going on and flew down. *If so, why hasn't she found me?*

*****

"Hi, are you Mrs. Becker?" asked the detective.

"Yes, I am. How may I help you?"

"May we come in? We need to ask you a few questions about your daughter and granddaughter."

"Sure, come in," answered Mrs. Becker nervously.

Holding a picture of Melissa and Kristen, the detectives asked if they were her daughter and granddaughter. After seeing the pictures of Melissa and Kristen, she knew this was really serious. She didn't want them to get in trouble but also knew she had to do the right thing. The last thing she wanted was to say something that might incriminate them.

She loved Lonnie but never knew he had a drinking problem. The thought of Melissa and Kristen going to jail worried her so badly that it made her heart feel weak. She knew she would surely die if that happened. She didn't know what to do. She really needed her husband. She felt so helpless.

The detectives asked general questions about Melissa. They wanted to know about her childhood and if she had any kind of anger issues. They also asked about Kristen's behavior. Mrs. Becker made her daughter's family seem to be just fine because as far as she knew, everything was fine.

She was surprised that the question of her having seen them didn't come up. She did not want to lie but also couldn't put them in jail.

"Mrs. Becker, I don't know if you know it, but your son-in-law, Lonnie Logan, was murdered in the Logans' house," explained the detective.

"Yes, I do know, but I don't know what happened," said Mrs. Becker nervously.

"We have Kristen in custody, but we still need to talk to Melissa."

She thought, *There is no way they can have Kristen without Melissa.* She wanted them to explain how that happened but didn't want them to think she knew more than she did.

"Would you try and call Melissa for us?" asked the detective.

"Sure, okay," answered Mrs. Becker with apprehension.

After several attempts, there was no answer, and Mrs. Becker was relieved that Melissa didn't answer.

"Okay, Mrs. Becker, here is my card. Please call if you talk to Melissa. We want to talk to her to see what she knows about what happened to Lonnie."

"Yes, I will," answered Mrs. Becker.

So the detectives left, and Melissa and Kristen came out of the back room.

"Melissa, can I talk to you for a minute?"

"Sure, Mom. Kristen, honey, please excuse us for a minute."

"Melissa, the detectives said they have Kristen in custody. How is that so?" asked Mrs. Becker, confused.

Melissa didn't know if she should tell her mom the truth or create more confusion by lying. "When I was pregnant, I was pregnant with twins. At that time, Lonnie had just gotten deployed, and I wasn't sure I could take care of two babies by myself," said Melissa.

"Honey, I would have helped you. You know that," stated Mrs. Becker.

"I know, Mom. But Dad was sick, and Lonnie was an alcoholic and very abusive," explained Melissa.

*****

The phone rang, and it was Mr. Hartley, Susanna's attorney. He explained who he was and that he was representing Susanna Logan Ramulla in a murder case. He also explained that Susanna claimed to be the daughter of Melissa Logan and had the evidence to prove it. Mrs. Becker thought that his story confirmed what she had just heard from Melissa, but she was still confused.

Mr. Hartley continued to say that Susanna was searching for her biological parents when she walked into a crime scene, and the detectives thought she was Kristen because they looked so much alike. She was arrested and taken to jail.

Mrs. Becker knew she couldn't let that innocent girl be held accountable for this terrible mistake. Mr. Hartley asked Mrs. Becker to please have Melissa and Kristen come forth and tell the detectives what happened.

"Mrs. Becker, the trial starts in two days, so please have your daughter and granddaughter do the right thing."

"Okay, I will talk to them," Mrs. Becker assured him.

Now that Mrs. Becker knew what she thought was as close to the truth as she was going to get, she told Melissa she had to go and tell the truth.

Melissa knew she had to go free Susanna. In her mind, she could make up to Susanna for giving her away at birth.

Melissa explained it all to Kristen, and she took it well but was mostly excited to hear that Susanna was her sister.

*****

Susanna was sitting there with her attorney, Mr. Hartley. She never thought she could ever be in this much trouble. She continued to look around her to see a familiar face.

"All rise," stated the bailiff as Judge Price approached his chair.

"Okay, you may be seated," instructed the judge. "This is the murder trial of the state of North Carolina versus Susanna Ramulla. Prosecution, are you ready?"

"Yes, we are."

"Defense, are you ready?"

"Yes, we are," stated Mr. Hartley.

The doors opened, and in came Melissa and Kristen. Kristen sat down, and Melissa proceeded to the defense table.

"I'm sorry to interrupt, but I'm the real murderer, not my daughter," stated Melissa.

The judge asked, "Who are you?"

"My name is Melissa Logan, the biological mother of Susanna Ramulla. I delivered the blow to the back of my husband's head with a golf club. I killed Lonnie Logan," she explained with tears.

Kristen backed her mother's confession.

Susanna was set free. Melissa went to jail and was later acquitted based on self-defense. The mother, sister, and daughter relationships began and grew stronger throughout the years.